A NOVEL IN NINE LETTERS

_____

BY

FYODOR DOSTOEVSKY

First Published in 1847

British Library Cataloguing-in-Publication Data
A catalogue record for this book is available
from the British Library

CONTENTS

FYODOR DOSTOEVSKY

Fyodor Mikhailovich Dostoevsky was born in Moscow, as the second son of a former army doctor. Raised within the grounds of the Mariinsky hospital, at an early age he was introduced to English, French, German and Russian literature, as well as to fairy-tales and legends. He was educated at home and at a private school, but shortly after the death of his mother in 1837, he was sent to St. Petersburg, where he entered the Army Engineering College.

In 1839 Dostoevsky's father died. A year later, Dostoevsky graduated as a military engineer, but resigned in 1844 to devote himself to writing. While earning money from translations, he wrote his first novel, *Poor Folk*, which appeared in 1846. It was followed by *The Double* (1846), which depicted a man who was haunted by a look-alike who eventually usurps his position.

In 1846, Dostoevsky joined a group of utopian socialists. He was arrested in 1849 and sentenced to death. After a mock execution, his sentence was reduced to imprisonment in Siberia. Dostoevsky spent four years in hard labour – ten years later, he would turn these experiences into *The House of the Dead* (1860). Upon his release, he joined the army in Semipalatinsk (North-East Kazakhstan), where he remained for a further four years.

Dostoevsky returned to St. Petersburg in 1854. Three years later, he married Maria Isaev, a 29-year old widow. He resigned from the army in 1859, and focussed once more on writing. Between the years 1861 and 1863 he served as editor of the monthly periodical *Time*, which was later suppressed because of an article on the Polish uprising.

In 1864-65 his wife and brother died and Dostoevsky was burdened with debts. The situation was made worse by his own lifelong gambling addiction. From the turmoil of the 1860s emerged his classic *Notes from the Underground* (1864), a psychological study of a social outcast seeking spiritual rebirth. The novel marked a watershed in Dostoevsky's artistic development.

Notes from the Underground (1864) was followed by Dostoevsky's most famous work, *Crime and Punishment* (1866). An account of an individual's fall and redemption, and an implicit critique of nihilism, it is now regarded as one of the greatest works of Russian literature. Two years later *The Idiot* (1868) was published, and three years after that came *The Possessed,* (1871) an exploration of philosophical nihilism.

In 1867 Dostoevsky married Anna Snitkin, his 22-year old stenographer. They travelled abroad and returned in 1871. By the time the *The Brothers Karamazov* was published, between 1879-80, Dostoevsky was recognized in his own country as one of its great writers. However, having suffered from a fragile mental disposition his whole life, Dostoevsky began to succumb to larger periods of mania and rage. After a particularly bad epileptic fit, he died in St. Petersburg in early 1881, aged 59.

Together with Leo Tolstoy, Dostoevsky is now regarded as one of the greatest and most influential novelists in all of Russian literature. His books have been translated into more than 170 languages and have sold around 15 million copies.

1

(FROM PYOTR IVANITCH TO IVAN PETROVITCH)

DEAR SIR AND MOST PRECIOUS FRIEND, IVAN PETROVITCH,

For the last two days I have been, I may say, in pursuit of you, my friend, having to talk over most urgent business with you, and I cannot come across you anywhere. Yesterday, while we were at Semyon Alexeyitch's, my wife made a very good joke about you, saying that Tatyana Petrovna and you were a pair of birds always on the wing. You have not been married three months and you already neglect your domestic hearth. We all laughed heartily—from our genuine kindly feeling for you, of course—but, joking apart, my precious friend, you have given me a lot of trouble. Semyon Alexeyitch said to me that you might be going to the ball at the Social Union's club! Leaving my wife with Semyon Alexeyitch's good lady, I flew off to the Social Union. It was funny and tragic! Fancy my position! Me at the ball—and alone, without my wife! Ivan Andreyitch meeting me in the porter's lodge and seeing me alone, at once concluded (the rascal!) that I had a passion for dances, and taking me by the arm, wanted to drag me off by force to a dancing class, saying that it was too crowded at the Social Union, that an ardent spirit had not room to turn, and that his head ached from the patchouli and mignonette. I found neither you, nor Tatyana Petrovna. Ivan Andreyitch vowed and declared that you would be at *Woe from Wit*, at the Alexandrinsky theatre.

I flew off to the Alexandrinsky theatre: you were not there

either. This morning I expected to find you at Tchistoganov's—no sign of you there. Tchistoganov sent to the Perepalkins'—the same thing there. In fact, I am quite worn out; you can judge how much trouble I have taken! Now I am writing to you (there is nothing else I can do). My business is by no means a literary one (you understand me?); it would be better to meet face to face, it is extremely necessary to discuss something with you and as quickly as possible, and so I beg you to come to us today with Tatyana Petrovna to tea and for a chat in the evening. My Anna Mihalovna will be extremely pleased to see you. You will truly, as they say, oblige me to my dying day. By the way, my precious friend—since I have taken up my pen I'll go into all I have against you—I have a slight complaint I must make; in fact, I must reproach you, my worthy friend, for an apparently very innocent little trick which you have played at my expense. . . . You are a rascal, a man without conscience. About the middle of last month, you brought into my house an acquaintance of yours, Yevgeny Nikolaitch; you vouched for him by your friendly and, for me, of course, sacred recommendation; I rejoiced at the opportunity of receiving the young man with open arms, and when I did so I put my head in a noose. A noose it hardly is, but it has turned out a pretty business. I have not time now to explain, and indeed it is an awkward thing to do in writing, only a very humble request to you, my malicious friend: could you not somehow very delicately, in passing, drop a hint into the young man's ear that there are a great many houses in the metropolis besides ours? It's more than I can stand, my dear fellow! We fall at your feet, as our friend Semyonovitch says. I will tell you all about it when we meet. I don't mean to say that the young man has sinned against good manners, or is lacking in spiritual qualities, or is not up to the mark in some other way. On the contrary, he is an amiable and pleasant fellow; but wait, we shall meet; meanwhile if you see him, for goodness' sake whisper a hint to him, my good friend. I would do it myself, but you know what I am, I simply can't, and that's all about it. You introduced him. But I will explain myself more fully this evening, anyway.

Now good-bye. I remain, etc.

P.S.—My little boy has been ailing for the last week, and gets worse and worse every day; he is cutting his poor little teeth. My wife is nursing him all the time, and is depressed, poor thing. Be sure to come, you will give us real pleasure, my precious friend.

2

(FROM IVAN PETROVITCH TO PYOTR IVANITCH)

DEAR SIR, PYOTR IVANITCH!

I got your letter yesterday, I read it and was perplexed. You looked for me, goodness knows where, and I was simply at home. Till ten o'clock I was expecting Ivan Ivanitch Tolokonov. At once on getting your letter I set out with my wife, I went to the expense of taking a cab, and reached your house about half-past six. You were not at home, but we were met by your wife. I waited to see you till half-past ten, I could not stay later. I set off with my wife, went to the expense of a cab again, saw her home, and went on myself to the Perepalkins', thinking I might meet you there, but again I was out in my reckoning. When I get home I did not sleep all night, I felt uneasy; in the morning I drove round to you three times, at nine, at ten and at eleven; three times I went to the expense of a cab, and again you left me in the lurch.

I read your letter and was amazed. You write about Yevgeny Nikolaitch, beg me to whisper some hint, and do not tell me what about. I commend your caution, but all letters are not alike, and I don't give documents of importance to my wife for curl-papers. I am puzzled, in fact, to know with what motive you wrote all this to me. However, if it comes to that, why should I meddle in the matter? I don't poke my nose into other people's business. You can be not at home to him; I only see that I must have a brief and decisive explanation with you, and, moreover, time is passing. And I am in straits and don't know what to do if you are going to neglect the terms of our agreement. A journey for nothing; a journey costs something, too, and my wife's whining for me to get her a velvet mantle of the latest fashion. About Yevgeny Nikolaitch I hasten to mention that when I was at Pavel Semyonovitch Perepalkin's yesterday I made inquiries without loss of time. He has five hundred serfs in the province of Yaroslav, and he has expectations from his grandmother of an estate of three hundred serfs near Moscow. How much money he has I cannot tell; I think you ought to know that better. I beg you once for all to appoint a place where I can meet you. You met Ivan Andreyitch yesterday, and you write that he told you that I was at the Alexandrinsky theatre with my wife. I write, that he is a liar, and it shows how little he is to be trusted in such cases, that only the day before yesterday he did his grandmother out of eight hundred roubles. I have the honour to remain, etc.

P.S.—My wife is going to have a baby; she is nervous about it and feels depressed at times. At the theatre they sometimes have fire-arms going off and sham thunderstorms. And so for fear of a shock to my wife's nerves I do not take her to the theatre. I have no great partiality for the theatre myself.

3

_____

(FROM PYOTR IVANITCH TO IVAN PETROVITCH)

MY PRECIOUS FRIEND, IVAN PETROVITCH,

I am to blame, to blame, a thousand times to blame, but I hasten to defend myself. Between five and six yesterday, just as we were talking of you with the warmest affection, a messenger from Uncle Stepan Alexeyitch galloped up with the news that my aunt was very bad. Being afraid of alarming my wife, I did not say a word of this to her, but on the pretext of other urgent business I drove off to my aunt's house. I found her almost dying. Just at five o'clock she had had a stroke, the third she has had in the last two years. Karl Fyodoritch, their family doctor, told us that she might not live through the night. You can judge of my position, dearest friend. We were on our legs all night in grief and anxiety. It was not till morning that, utterly exhausted and overcome by moral and physical weakness, I lay down on the sofa; I forgot to tell them to wake me, and only woke at half-past eleven. My aunt was better. I drove home to my wife. She, poor thing, was quite worn out expecting me. I snatched a bite of something, embraced my little boy, reassured my wife and set off to call on you. You were not at home. At your flat I found Yevgeny Nikolaitch. When I got home I took up a pen, and here I am writing to you. Don't grumble and be cross to me, my true friend. Beat me, chop my guilty head off my shoulders, but don't deprive me of your affection. From your wife I learned that you will be at the Slavyanovs' this evening. I will certainly be there. I look forward with the greatest impatience to seeing you.

I remain, etc.

P.S.—We are in perfect despair about our little boy. Karl Fyodoritch prescribes rhubarb. He moans. Yesterday he did not know any one. This morning he did know us, and began lisping papa, mamma, boo. . . . My wife was in tears the whole morning.

4

(FROM IVAN PETROVITCH TO PYOTR IVANITCH)

MY DEAR SIR, PYOTR IVANITCH!

I am writing to you, in your room, at your bureau; and before taking up my pen, I have been waiting for more than two and a half hours for you. Now allow me to tell you straight out, Pyotr Ivanitch, my frank opinion about this shabby incident. From your last letter I gathered that you were expected at the Slavyanovs', that you were inviting me to go there; I turned up, I stayed for five hours and there was no sign of you. Why, am I to be made a laughing-stock to people, do you suppose? Excuse me, my dear sir . . . I came to you this morning, I hoped to find you, not imitating certain deceitful persons who look for people, God knows where, when they can be found at home at any suitably chosen time. There is no sign of you at home. I don't know what restrains me from telling you now the whole harsh truth. I will only say that I see you seem to be going back on your bargain regarding our agreement. And only now reflecting on the whole affair, I cannot but confess that I am absolutely astounded at the artful workings of your mind. I see clearly now that you have been cherishing your unfriendly design for a long time. This supposition of mine is confirmed by the fact that last week in an almost unpardonable way you took possession of that letter of yours addressed to me, in which you laid down yourself, though rather vaguely and incoherently, the terms of our agreement in regard to a circumstance of which I need not remind you. You are afraid of documents, you destroy them, and you try to make a fool of me. But I won't allow myself to be made a fool of, for no one has ever considered me one hitherto, and every one has thought well of me in that respect. I am opening my eyes. You try and put me off, confuse me with talk of Yevgeny Nikolaitch, and when with your letter of the seventh of this month, which I am still at a loss to understand, I seek a personal explanation from you, you make humbugging appointments, while you keep out of the way. Surely you do not suppose, sir, that I am not equal to noticing all this? You promised to reward me for my services, of which you are very well aware, in the way of introducing various persons, and at the same time, and I don't know how you do it, you contrive to borrow money from me in considerable sums without giving a receipt, as happened no longer ago than last week. Now, having got the money, you keep out of the way, and what's more, you repudiate the service I have done you in regard to Yevgeny Nikolaitch. You are probably reckoning on my speedy departure to Simbirsk, and hoping I may not have time to settle your business. But I assure you solemnly and testify on my word of honour that if it comes to that, I am prepared to spend two more months in Petersburg expressly to carry through my business, to attain my objects, and to get hold of you. For I, too, on occasion know how to get the better of people. In conclusion, I beg to inform you that if you do not give me a satisfactory explanation today, first in writing, and then personally face to face, and do not make a fresh statement in your letter of the chief points of the agreement existing between us, and do not explain fully your views in regard to Yevgeny Nikolaitch, I shall be compelled to have recourse to measures that will be highly unpleasant to you, and indeed repugnant to me also.

Allow me to remain, etc.

5

(FROM PYOTR IVANITCH TO IVAN PETROVITCH)

November 11.

MY DEAR AND HONOURED FRIEND, IVAN PETROVITCH!

I was cut to the heart by your letter. I wonder you were not ashamed, my dear but unjust friend, to behave like this to one of your most devoted friends. Why be in such a hurry, and without explaining things fully, wound me with such insulting suspicions? But I hasten to reply to your charges. You did not find me yesterday, Ivan Petrovitch, because I was suddenly and quite unexpectedly called away to a death-bed. My aunt, Yefimya Nikolaevna, passed away yesterday evening at eleven o'clock in the night. By the general consent of the relatives I was selected to make the arrangements for the sad and sorrowful ceremony. I had so much to do that I had not time to see you this morning, nor even to send you a line. I am grieved to the heart at the misunderstanding which has arisen between us. My words about Yevgeny Nikolaitch uttered casually and in jest you have taken in quite a wrong sense, and have ascribed to them a meaning deeply offensive to me. You refer to money and express your anxiety about it. But without wasting words I am ready to satisfy all your claims and demands, though I must remind you that the three hundred and fifty roubles I had from you last week were in accordance with a certain agreement and not by way of a loan. In the latter case there would certainly have been a receipt. I will not condescend to discuss the other points mentioned in your letter. I see that it is a misunderstanding. I see it is your habitual hastiness, hot temper and obstinacy. I know that your goodheartedness and open character will not allow doubts to persist in your heart, and that you will be, in fact, the first to hold out your hand to me. You are mistaken, Ivan Petrovitch, you are greatly mistaken!

Although your letter has deeply wounded me, I should be prepared even today to come to you and apologise, but I have been since yesterday in such a rush and flurry that I am utterly exhausted and can scarcely stand on my feet. To complete my troubles, my wife is laid up; I am afraid she is seriously ill. Our little boy, thank God, is better; but I must lay down my pen, I have a mass of things to do and they are urgent. Allow me, my dear friend, to remain, etc.

6

(FROM IVAN PETROVITCH TO PYOTR IVANITCH)

November 14.

DEAR SIR, PYOTR IVANITCH!

I have been waiting for three days, I tried to make a profitable use of them—meanwhile I feel that politeness and good manners are the greatest of ornaments for every one. Since my last letter of the tenth of this month, I have neither by word nor deed reminded you of my existence, partly in order to allow you undisturbed to perform the duty of a Christian in regard to your aunt, partly because I needed the time for certain considerations and investigations in regard to a business you know of. Now I hasten to explain myself to you in the most thoroughgoing and decisive manner.

I frankly confess that on reading your first two letters I seriously supposed that you did not understand what I wanted; that was how it was that I rather sought an interview with you and explanations face to face. I was afraid of writing, and blamed myself for lack of clearness in the expression of my thoughts on paper. You are aware that I have not the advantages of education and good manners, and that I shun a hollow show of gentility because I have learned from bitter experience how misleading appearances often are, and that a snake sometimes lies hidden under flowers. But you understood me; you did not answer me as you should have done because, in the treachery of your heart, you had planned beforehand to be faithless to your word of honour and to the friendly relations existing between us. You have proved this absolutely by your abominable conduct towards me of late, which is fatal to my interests, which I did not expect and which I refused to believe till the present moment. From the very beginning of our acquaintance you captivated me by your clever manners, by the subtlety of your behaviour, your knowledge of affairs and the advantages to be gained by association with you. I imagined that I had found a true friend and well-wisher. Now I recognise clearly that there are many people who under a flattering and brilliant exterior hide venom in their hearts, who use their cleverness to weave snares for their neighbour and for unpardonable deception, and so are afraid of pen and paper, and at the same time use their fine language not for the benefit of their neighbour and their country, but to drug and bewitch the reason of those who have entered into business relations of any sort with them. Your treachery to me, my dear sir, can be clearly seen from what follows.

In the first place, when, in the clear and distinct terms of my letter, I described my position, sir, and at the same time asked you in my first letter what you meant by certain expressions and intentions of yours, principally in regard to Yevgeny Nikolaitch, you tried for the most part to avoid answering, and confounding me by doubts and suspicions, you calmly put the subject aside. Then after treating me in a way which cannot be described by any seemly word, you began writing that you were wounded. Pray, what am I to call that, sir? Then when every minute was precious to me and when you had set me running after you all over the town, you wrote, pretending personal friendship, letters in which, intentionally avoiding all mention of business, you spoke of utterly irrelevant matters; to wit, of the illnesses of your good lady for whom I have, in any case, every respect, and of how your baby had been dosed with rhubarb and was cutting a tooth. All this you alluded to in every letter with a disgusting regularity that was insulting to me. Of course I am prepared to admit that a father's heart may be torn by the sufferings of his babe, but why make mention of this when something different, far more important and interesting, was needed? I endured it in silence, but now when time has elapsed I think it my duty to explain myself. Finally, treacherously deceiving me several times by making humbugging appointments, you tried, it seems, to make me play the part of a fool and a laughing-stock for you, which I never intend to be. Then after first inviting me and thoroughly deceiving me, you informed me that you were called away to your suffering aunt who had had a stroke, precisely at five o'clock as you stated with shameful exactitude. Luckily for me, sir, in the course of these three days I have succeeded in making inquiries and have learnt from them that your aunt had a stroke on the day before the seventh not long before midnight. From this fact I see that you have made use of sacred family relations in order to deceive persons in no way concerned with them. Finally, in your last letter you mention the death of your relatives as though it had taken place precisely at the time when I was to have visited you to consult about various business matters. But here the vileness of your arts and calculations exceeds all belief, for from trustworthy information which I was able by a lucky chance to obtain just in the nick of time, I have found out that your aunt died twenty-four hours later than the time you so impiously fixed for her decease in your letter. I shall never have done if I enumerate all the signs by which I have discovered your treachery in regard to me. It is sufficient, indeed, for any impartial observer that in every letter you style me, your true friend, and call me all sorts of polite names, which you do, to the best of my belief, for no other object than to put my conscience to sleep.

I have come now to your principal act of deceit and treachery in regard to me, to wit, your continual silence of late in regard to everything concerning our common interests, in regard to your wicked theft of the letter in which you stated, though in language somewhat obscure and not perfectly intelligible to me, our mutual agreements, your barbarous forcible loan of three hundred and fifty roubles which you borrowed from me as your partner without giving any receipt, and finally, your abominable slanders of our common acquaintance, Yevgeny Nikolaitch. I see clearly now that you meant to show me that he was, if you will allow me to say so, like a billy-goat, good for neither milk nor wool, that he was neither one thing nor the other, neither fish nor flesh, which you put down as a vice in him in your letter of the sixth instant. I knew Yevgeny Nikolaitch as a modest and well-behaved young man, whereby he may well attract, gain and deserve respect in society. I know also that every evening for the last fortnight you've put into your pocket dozens and sometimes even hundreds of roubles, playing games of chance with Yevgeny Nikolaitch. Now you disavow all this, and not only refuse to compensate me for what I have suffered, but have even appropriated money belonging to me, tempting me by suggestions that I should be partner in the affair, and luring me with various advantages which were to accrue. After having appropriated, in a most illegal way, money of mine and of Yevgeny Nikolaitch's, you decline to compensate me, resorting for that object to calumny with which you have unjustifiably blackened in my eyes a man whom I, by my efforts and exertions, introduced into your house. While on the contrary, from what I hear from your friends, you are still almost slobbering over him, and give out to the whole world that he is your dearest friend, though there is no one in the world such a fool as not to guess at once what your designs are aiming at and what your friendly relations really mean. I should say that they mean deceit, treachery, forgetfulness of human duties and proprieties, contrary to the law of God and vicious in every way. I take myself as a proof and example. In what way have I offended you and why have you treated me in this godless fashion?

I will end my letter. I have explained myself. Now in conclusion. If, sir, you do not in the shortest possible time after receiving this letter return me in full, first, the three hundred and fifty roubles I gave you, and, secondly, all the sums that should come to me according to your promise, I will have recourse to every possible means to compel you to return it, even to open force, secondly to the protection of the laws, and finally I beg to inform you that I am in possession of facts, which, if they remain in the hands of your humble servant, may ruin and disgrace your name in the eyes of all the world. Allow me to remain, etc.

7

(FROM PYOTR IVANITCH TO IVAN PETROVITCH)

November 15.

IVAN PETROVITCH!

When I received your vulgar and at the same time queer letter, my impulse for the first minute was to tear it into shreds, but I have preserved it as a curiosity. I do, however, sincerely regret our misunderstandings and unpleasant relations. I did not mean to answer you. But I am compelled by necessity. I must in these lines inform you that it would be very unpleasant for me to see you in my house at any time; my wife feels the same: she is in delicate health and the smell of tar upsets her. My wife sends your wife the book, *Don Quixote de la Mancha*, with her sincere thanks. As for the galoshes you say you left behind here on your last visit, I must regretfully inform you that they are nowhere to be found. They are still being looked for; but if they do not turn up, then I will buy you a new pair.

I have the honour to remain your sincere friend,

8

On the sixteenth of November, Pyotr Ivanitch received by post two letters addressed to him. Opening the first envelope, he took out a carefully folded note on pale pink paper. The handwriting was his wife's. It was addressed to Yevgeny Nikolaitch and dated November the second. There was nothing else in the envelope. Pyotr Ivanitch read:

DEAR EUGÈNE,

Yesterday was utterly impossible. My husband was at home the whole evening. Be sure to come tomorrow punctually at eleven. At half-past ten my husband is going to Tsarskoe and not coming back till evening. I was in a rage all night. Thank you for sending me the information and the correspondence. What a lot of paper. Did she really write all that? She has style though; many thanks, dear; I see that you love me. Don't be angry, but, for goodness sake, come tomorrow.

A.

Pyotr Ivanitch tore open the other letter:

PYOTR IVANITCH,

I should never have set foot again in your house anyway; you need not have troubled to soil paper about it.

Next week I am going to Simbirsk. Yevgany Nikolaitch remains your precious and beloved friend. I wish you luck, and don't trouble about the galoshes.

9

On the seventeenth of November Ivan Petrovitch received by post two letters addressed to him. Opening the first letter, he took out a hasty and carelessly written note. The handwriting was his wife's; it was addressed to Yevgeny Nikolaitch, and dated August the fourth. There was nothing else in the envelope. Ivan Petrovitch read:

Good-bye, good-bye, Yevgeny Nikolaitch! The Lord reward you for this too. May you be happy, but my lot is bitter, terribly bitter! It is your choice. If it had not been for my aunt I should not have put such trust in you. Do not laugh at me nor at my aunt. To-morrow is our wedding. Aunt is relieved that a good man has been found, and that he will take me without a dowry. I took a good look at him for the first time today. He seems good-natured. They are hurrying me. Farewell, farewell. . . . My darling!! Think of me sometimes; I shall never forget you. Farewell! I sign this last like my first letter, do you remember?

TATYANA.

The second letter was as follows:

IVAN PETROVITCH,

To-morrow you will receive a new pair of galoshes. It is not my habit to filch from other men's pockets, and I am not fond of picking up all sorts of rubbish in the streets.

Yevgeny Nikolaitch is going to Simbirsk in a day or two on his grandfather's business, and he has asked me to find a travelling companion for him; wouldn't you like to take him with you?

Printed in Great Britain
by Amazon

37110934R00020